Molly Maybe
and the

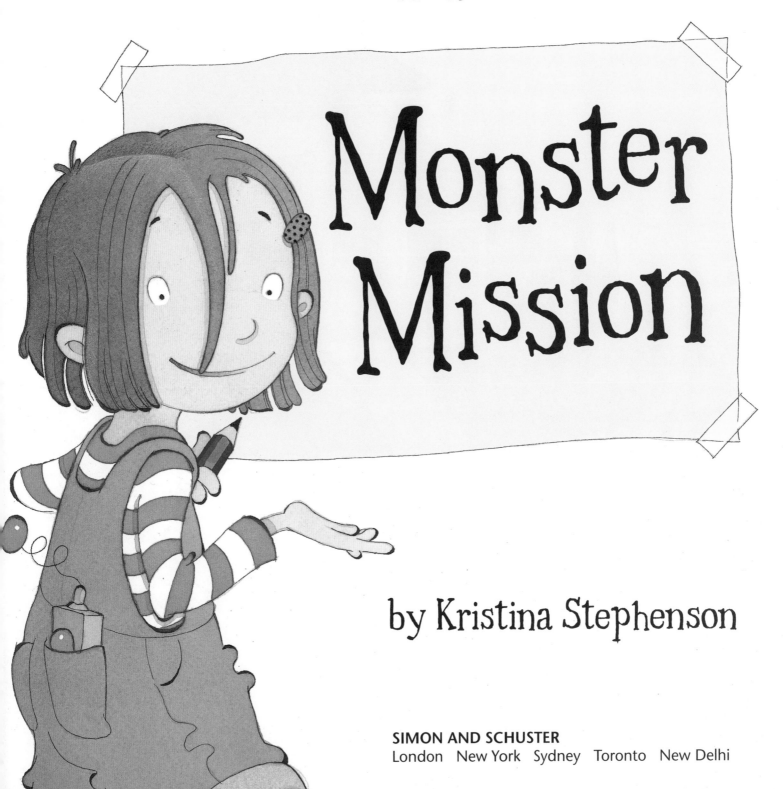

Monster Mission

by Kristina Stephenson

SIMON AND SCHUSTER
London New York Sydney Toronto New Delhi

This is Smallsbury.
It's a sleepy little town where
nothing much ever happens.

At least that's how it might seem.

Molly Maybe

For my amazing mum,
Karen Stephenson,
with all my love X

SIMON AND SCHUSTER
First published in Great Britain in 2015 by
Simon and Schuster UK Ltd, 1st Floor, 222 Gray's Inn Road, London WC1X 8HB
This edition published 2016
A CBS Company
Text and illustrations copyright © 2015 Kristina Stephenson
The right of Kristina Stephenson to be identified as the author and illustrator of this work
has been asserted by her in accordance with the Copyright, Designs and Patents Act, 1988
All rights reserved, including the right of reproduction in whole or in part in any form
A CIP catalogue record for this book is available from the British Library upon request
978-1-4711-8186-3 (PB)
978-1-4711-2108-1 (eBook)
Printed in China
1 3 5 7 9 10 8 6 4 2

In this snoringly, boringly ordinary place, Molly Maybe was up in her tree house with her dog by her side.

Next door, Molly's neighbour, Mr Bottomly Brown, was digging a pond in his garden when he suddenly found something rather peculiar.

'Look at that, Waggy Burns,' said Molly. 'Whatever could it be?'

Then, three days later, Molly and Waggy heard a terrible roar.

It was Mr Bottomly Brown, shouting.

'Look at my perfect lawn!
Pesky moles have been digging holes.'

Molly shook her head.
'Moles?' she said. 'I don't think so.'
And that's when she spotted . . .

the claw.

'I knew it,' said Molly. 'There are monsters at work and we need to find out why. Time to go underground, Waggy Burns!'

Waggy wiggled his wiry whiskers and waggled off to fetch his special Walkie-Talkie Collar.

Then they opened a door in the tree house floor.

You see, Molly's tree house was no ORDINARY tree house. Inside it was the best-kept secret in Smallsbury. It led to a magical monster world and Molly's marvellous Mundervator was the only way to get there.

round the bend,

and into . . .

Down,

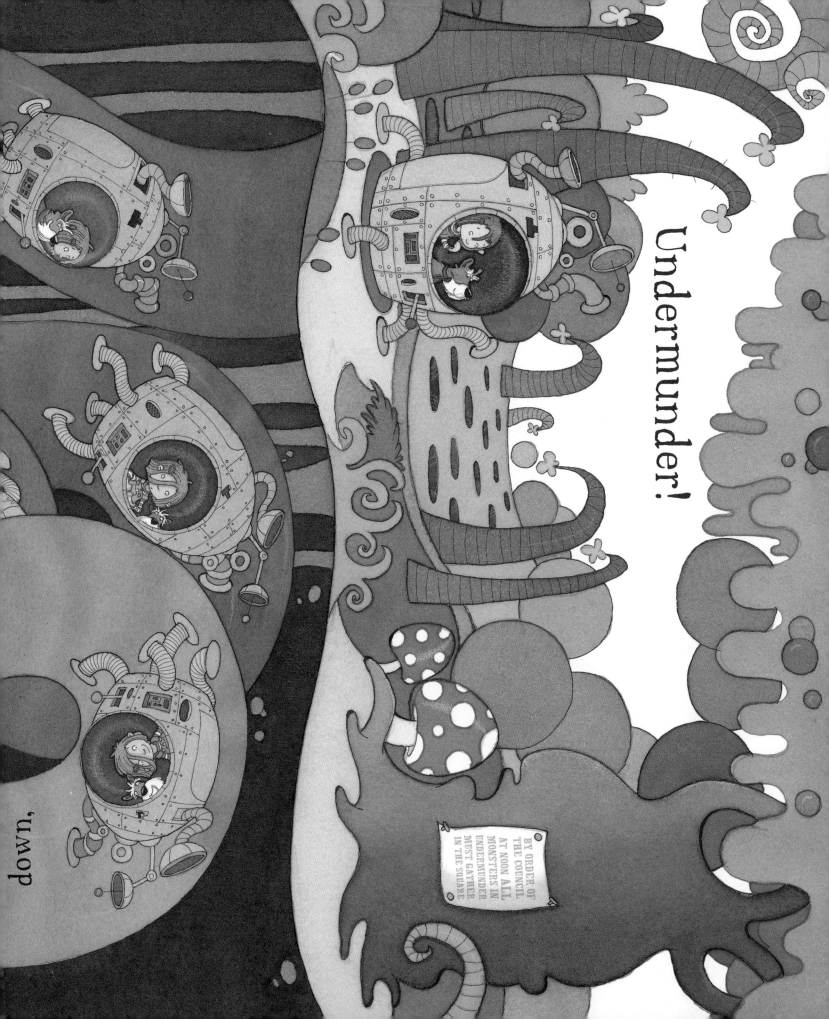

down,

Undermunder!

BY ORDER OF
THE COUNCIL,
AT NOON ALL
MONSTERS IN
UNDERMUNDER
MUST GATHER
IN THE SQUARE

Clunk! The Mundervator dropped them in the middle of the Murbling Wood. 'Odd!' said Molly. 'I wonder why the Mundervator decided to bring us here?'

'Woof, woof, woof!' said Waggy.
'Oops,' said Molly. 'I nearly forgot!'
And she turned on Waggy's collar.

'My canine calculations tell me
we need to go to town,' he said
and read:

BY ORDER OF
THE COUNCIL
AT NOON **ALL**
MONSTERS IN
UNDERMUNDER
MUST GATHER
IN THE SQUARE

'Then that's where we'll find our
lawn-destroying monster,'
said Molly with a grin.

Waggy was right.
In a hustle and bustle of monster mayhem,
there were monsters EVERYWHERE.

'Golly,' said Molly when she saw them all.
'How will we find the right one?'

But before Waggy Burns
could speak...

CREAK! The doors of the town hall opened and everyone turned to see the Monster Meister of Undermunder.

'Fellow monsters!' he said. 'The Mydol Idol – the monster mascot that has always stood in this Square – HAS BEEN STOLEN!'

The monsters gasped.

'If it is returned by midnight,' the Meister continued, 'nothing more will be said. But the thief will be banished from Undermunder if I have to seek him out instead.'

As the Meister was speaking, Molly noticed that the biggest, hairiest, scariest monster was looking shiftily down at the floor. And not only that. He had mud all over his claws.

'Golly,' said Molly. 'Could he be the thief and the dirt-digging monster?'

Waggy Burns wiggled his whiskers. 'Only one way to find out!' he said.

So they followed the monster out of town,
making sure he didn't see them.

He mumbled and grumbled and muttered
as he went.

'Got to hurry! Got to hurry!' he said, over and over again,
as he led them back along the track and into . . .

... the Murbling Wood.

Molly and Waggy peeped round a tree and watched him dig a hole.

'It's got to be here! It's got to be here!' muttered the monster.

Waggy's whiskers wiggled again as he whispered to Molly Maybe. 'Doggy deduction leads me to believe this monster is searching for something and he's been digging holes from Undermunder to Mr Bottomly Brown's perfect lawn.'

'I said it wasn't moles!' squealed Molly, bouncing about with glee.

But she didn't see the monster turn and make his way towards them. He was huge, hairy, and . . .

... not at **all** scary.

'I'm a silly old Dappity-Doofer,' he said. 'I took the Mydol Idol. I buried it somewhere here – I think – and I came back to get it last night.

I thought that if I hid it, and pretended to find it, the others would think I was clever and not just a silly old monster. But my plan has gone wrong! I've dug and dug all over the place and the Mydol Idol has GONE.'

'Gracious good golly!' said Molly Maybe. 'I know where it is!'

She opened the door of the Mundervator and pushed the monster in. Heeeaaave.

Down,

down,

round the bend and back to . . .

... Molly's tree house, where the Dappity-Doofer
was thrilled to see the Mydol Idol next door.
'Let's get it! Let's get it!' he said to Molly.
But Waggy wasn't so sure.
'Woof!' he warned. (His collar only worked in Undermunder.)

And Molly Maybe saw ...

THE VECTOR SPECTOR MOLE DETECTOR
MODEL 303

Screeches if **anything** touches your lawn
MONEY BACK GUARANTEE!

'Drat!' said Molly. 'We can't!
Mr Bottomly Brown will hear us.'

Up in the tree house they sat and thought.

Three mugs of cocoa later ...
'I've got it!' said Molly. 'The perfect plan!
But there's an awful lot to do.

We need to find some rope, a big hook, a catapult
and a really "special something" to put in place
of the Mydol Idol so Mr Bottomly Brown doesn't
notice it's gone.'

It took the rest of the day to get
ready but when everyone in
Smallsbury had gone to bed,
it was time for the perfect plan.

But ...

'Gosh! What a long way down!' said Molly.
'Woof, woof, woof!' warned Waggy.

'You're right,' said Molly. 'It's much too dangerous.
So much for my perfect plan. But the Mydol Idol!
We're running out of time. Now what are we going to do?'

Dappity-Doofer
to the rescue!

With a wibble
and a wobble and
a WHOOAAHH, that
daring, dancing monster
scooped up the Mydol Idol.

In its place he left the "special
something" for Mr Bottomly Brown.

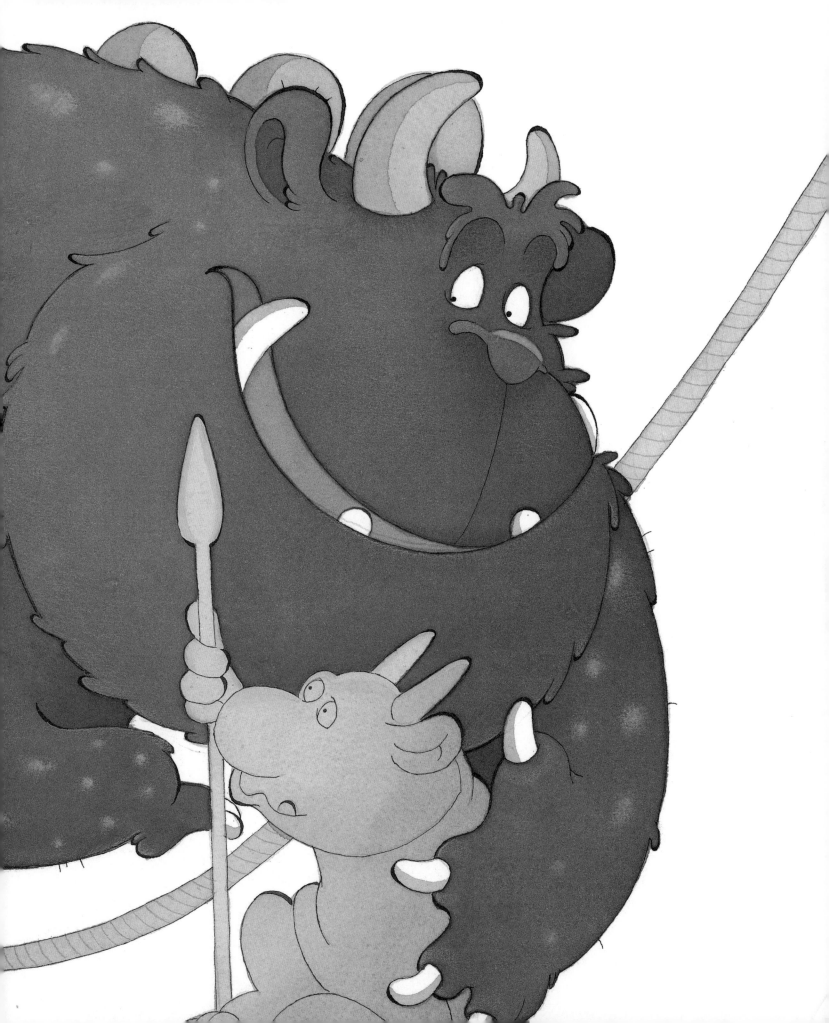

The next day, down in Undermunder,
the monsters were delighted to
see the Mydol Idol back in
its place as if nothing
had ever happened.

'Monster mission
accomplished,' said Molly.
Waggy wiggled his whiskers.

While, up in Smallsbury, Mr Bottomly Brown came out to admire his garden. Where . . .

. . . he found the "special something"!

But despite his appearance he is a charismatic villain whose wit and cleverness often make audiences laugh even as they are disgusted by his deeds.

Some people dispute Shakespeare's presentation of history and his depiction of a villainous and deformed Richard. They suggest he was writing with a heavy bias towards the Tudors. No one knows what really happened to the princes in the Tower – the twelve-year-old Edward and his brother the Duke of York. They certainly disappeared a month after Richard's coronation and the bones of two children found in the Tower of London in 1674 are thought to be the remains of the young princes.

Richard, however, is not the only suspect for their deaths. Some point out that Henry Tudor had just as much to gain from them being killed. Even though historians might protest Richard's innocence it remains Shakespeare's skilful presentation of the wicked king that is best known.

RICHARD III FACTS

Richard III has been simplified by:

✤   Colley Cibber in the 18th century in a version that was performed for 200 years.

✤   Laurence Olivier in his 1955 film that borrowed Cibber's lines.

✤   Richard Loncraine in the 1995 film starring Sir Ian McKellan that reset the story in the 1930s.